D1535405

THE
MUSHROOM
CENTER DISASTER

THE
MUSHROOM
CENTER DISASTER

N. M. Bodecker

Pictures by

Erik Blegvad

A MARGARET K. MCELDERRY BOOK

AN ALADDIN BOOK
Atheneum

With grateful acknowledgement to Robert Norton
for the layout of this book

Published by Atheneum
All rights reserved
Copyright © 1974 by N. M. Bodecker
Illustrations copyright © 1974 by Erik Blegvad
Published simultaneously in Canada by
McClelland & Stewart, Ltd.
Printed by The Murray Printing Company, Forge Village, Massachusetts
Bound by Connecticut Printers, Inc., Hartford, Connecticut
ISBN 0-689-70455-0
First Aladdin Edition

To Gertrude and Edric Weld

Deep in the woods, on the other side of the mountain, halfway between the brook and the pine trees, is a small rock no bigger than a robin's egg.

Next to the rock is an arrow, carved out of a pine needle, and a sign saying: To the Mushrooms. If you look carefully under the ferns where the arrow is pointing, you will see a narrow little path leading deeper into the woods. It is so narrow that two caterpillars couldn't pass each other on it, but smooth and tidy, as if someone had swept it with a dandelion down.

If you follow the path, through the Mole Hills, you come at last to a small clearing full of white mushrooms. The first mushroom on your left has a sign next to it saying:

MUSHROOMS FOR RENT

BY THE MONTH OR THE YEAR

INQUIRE WITHIN

It is quite the most inviting little mushroom ever, with brightly polished windows and a green front door with a brass knocker in the middle, just waiting for someone to knock.

It happened late one afternoon that a small brown beetle came down the path from the Mole Hills.

He was tired and dusty, for he had been traveling since early morning, and now he was looking for a place to stay. Nothing grand and fancy, mind you, just a snuggery of sorts, with an easy chair and a braided rug and a bed with a quilted comforter.

So when he came to the sign, "Mushrooms for Rent," he brushed the dust off his coat, combed his hair with his fingers, and tapped the door knocker briskly three times, like a man who had made up his mind and is not about to change it.

Almost instantly, there was a flutter of little feet from a corridor inside the mushroom, and a tiny voice said: "Just a moment, please."

After that, there was a rattling of keys, a snapping of locks, and a whole little string of "dear mes" and "Goodness graciouses" before the door finally opened, and the landlady—who happened to be a ladybug—came out and said, "This way please. The tea is on the table."

The table was set in a bay window overlooking a small garden full of cabbages and roses. Two arm-chairs were drawn up to the table, in the middle of which sat the teapot, surrounded by an expectant crowd of jam jars and honey pots and baskets of toast and crumpets.

For a long time, all the ladybug said was, "Do try this . . ." and, "Please have some of that . . ." and, "Just one more cup, Mr. Beetle."

And all the beetle said was, "Yes, please," and,

"Thank you," and, "I don't mind if I do."

When he had finished his fourth cup of tea and the last crumpet but one, he folded his napkin, leaned back in his chair, and enquired about the mushrooms for rent.

"Dear me," said the ladybug. "I haven't any. That is, right at this moment I don't. Perhaps I should have taken the sign in."

The brown beetle looked rather sad at this, but the ladybug poured him still another cup and said: "Of course, there *is* the guest mushroom. Not much of a place. All overgrown, I'm afraid. But if you like it, you are welcome to it for as long as you want."

So when they had finished their tea, they went out the back door, into the garden of cabbages and roses, through a small white gate, into another little garden

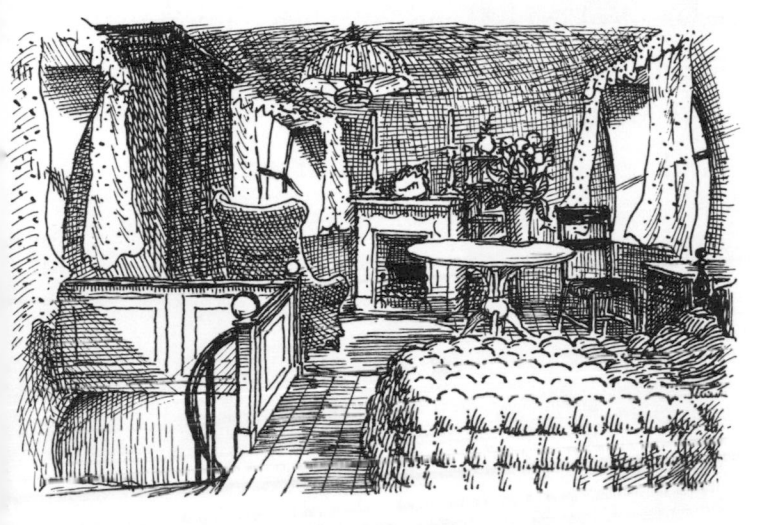

where the guest mushroom grew all by itself in a blaze of hollyhocks and morning glories. If you've ever wondered what a guest mushroom looks like inside—and who hasn't?—well, just listen.

Downstairs was a small circular front hall, with a hat rack and a spiral staircase. Upstairs was a larger circular room, with windows all around so that you could watch sunrise and sunset and everything in between without ever going outside. It had a large drowsy-looking bed with a quilted comforter. It had a braided rug and an easy chair, a fireplace, with two candlesticks and a seashell on the mantle, a what-not stand and a large, old-fashioned wardrobe.

"I wish it wasn't such an odd nook of a place," said the ladybug, when they had looked it over, "but I do hope you like it."

The beetle, who was quite overwhelmed and hadn't said a word for a long while, said simply, "I do." And that is how he came to live in Mushroom Center. When the disaster struck, they were all glad that he had come.

He lived quietly in his little round house, minding his own business and being as helpful as he could when someone needed him.

From his front windows he looked out on Caterpillar Walk, with its stately mushrooms and majestic lawns. From his back window he looked into Touchwood Close, a fussy little backwater, with quaint cottages and old-world gardens. One of his side windows looked into the Fern Woods. The other overlooked Mushroom Common, graced by a statue of a gnat crowning a mealybug with a wreath of laurel.

One by one he visited the other inhabitants of the village. He had lunch with the snail in "Mon Repose" and tea with the spider at "Webbwood." The caterpillar and her nephew gave him cucumber sandwiches in the garden at "Villa Alberdalf" (named after her dear departed parents Alberta and Alfred).

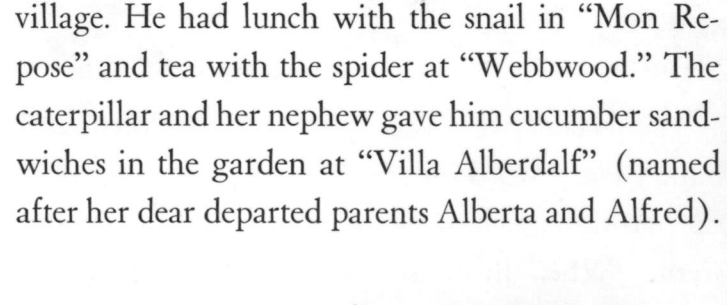

He had breakfast with the cricket in "Parson's Cottage," a candlelight supper (or so it seemed) with the firefly in the "Inglenook," and a late, quieting cup of chamomile tea with the moth at "Vale End," the last curious little cottage in Touch-wood Close.

This way time passed pleasantly enough. When he felt the need for things more exciting than cucumber sandwiches, he took to the river, shooting the rapids on a stick, or he took to the woods, hiking for days on end, encountering fierce tribes of aboriginal ants.

So the summer wore on, and one morning, when he stepped out into the crisp, clear sunshine, there was a touch of autumn in the air. That day he climbed the most precipitous of the Mole Hills to admire the view and enjoy a picnic lunch, alone with the sky and with his own far-reaching thoughts.

That evening he retired early. He put on his nightshirt, climbed into bed, and stretched himself on his back, looking at a crack in the ceiling. He thought how far away the sky had been that afternoon on top of the Mole Hill and how close the ceiling was now, and he tried to make it make some sense, but he couldn't. So he turned over to blow out the candle and, just as he blew, there was a crash! The candle went out, and the dark around him was full of bangs and clangs and rattles. The house shook, and something huge and odd went bump through the Fern Woods!

He sat up in bed, looking straight at the window in front of him, the one facing the woods. But before he could make out what was happening, whatever was happening *had* happened.

By the time he came out of his front door, the night was still and the sky was full of stars.

As he stood there on the front step in his nightshirt, with an unlit lantern in his hand, he wondered if anything had really happened, or if he had fallen asleep the moment he got into bed and dreamed the whole thing.

But as his eyes got used to the dark, he saw that something had indeed happened. Where the ladybug's house was supposed to be, it wasn't! In its place was a huge cylindrical object, tilting a little to the east and glinting faintly in the starlight.

He lit the lantern and shone it about him in the garden. There were splashes of red and ocher all over the place, the morning glories were torn and tangled, and when he felt his feet getting cold and looked down, he found himself standing in a large puddle of brown mustard—the kind that goes so nicely with grilled frankfurters.

He was not a beetle who scared easily, but even

his stout heart beat a little faster, as he stepped out of the mustard to wipe his feet on the lawn.

Whatever had happened was pretty peculiar.

He stood quietly for a moment, listening to the wind in the woods and the little sounds that were all around him.

A cricket chirped. Somewhere in the Close, a window banged against a wall.

Then quite near, someone said: "Dear me! What

21

a mess!" And the cylindrical thing (whatever it was) tilted a little farther to the east.

Without another moment's hesitation, the beetle picked up his lantern and strode briskly through the gate into the ladybug's garden.

The garden of cabbages and roses was worse than his own. There were splashes of red and ocher wherever he looked. The lawn was a tangle of long hideous plastic tubes, and "Fernview," the ladybug's mushroom, was lying on its side in a pile of dark

rubble smelling vaguely of barbecue sauce.

The cylindrical object that had knocked "Fernview" over looked even larger and more menacing when seen up close. It was covered with strange writing and outlandish signs.

He let his lantern shine here and there over the fallen house and ruined garden, calling softly: "Miss Ladybug! Miss Ladybug! Please! Where are you?" until the lantern showed her clinging to the chimney pot, smiling bravely and saying: "I'm all right.

Really I am. There has been some kind of commotion, but I'm quite all right."

The ladybug, when she came down from the chimney, was indeed all right— but Mushroom Center was not.

As they made their way into the Walk, they saw only ruin and destruction. The whole village seemed buried in U.F.R. (Unidentified Flying Rubbish)— odd lumps, puddles, and things that went crunch underfoot.

From every mushroom in the Walk and the Close came bewildered little figures in dressing gowns and slippers, carrying lamps and lanterns, picking their way through the rubble and heading for the Common.

The Common itself was blocked by a flying saucer from which spilled large hunks of lukewarm molten moon rock that smelled of cinnamon and turned out to be apple pie.

To you, perhaps, the remains of a picnic dropped somewhere in the woods doesn't mean much. But a mess is a mess, and to the people in Mushroom Center, this mess was a disaster.

They stood there on the Common, shivering a little in the night air, too sad to talk and too grown-up to cry. In a single moment, their beautiful little town had been turned into a dump. They no longer had lawns and flowerbeds, but puddles of catsup and ice cream, with cigarette butts and potato-chip chips stuck in them. Their houses were down, their fences broken, and their trim, happy, honeysuckled little gardens were smelling of salami and cheese and tuna fish salad.

They poked around in the rubbish a bit with their feet, but there really was nothing they could do except try to get some sleep. Some went to Snail's house and some went to Beetle's, the only two places left undamaged. It was a crowded night and not very comfortable. They tossed and turned, on sofas, on

chairs, and on floors, but at last they all slept.

And while they slept, the moon rose over the mountain, and Mushroom Center got its generous share of moonlight and deep blue shadows.

Early next morning, they went to look at the damage together. Everything looked worse in daylight than it had the night before.

They found more rubbish, more candy wrappers, more crumpled tinfoil, more bits and pieces of hamburgers and hard-boiled eggs and cottage cheese. They found a pickle stuck in Moth's chimney and Cricket's chimney stuck in an egg roll.

There were piles of tuna fish salad and coleslaw in the Close and a chunk of knackwurst in Caterpillar's greenhouse. The thing that had gone bump through the Fern Woods turned out to be an empty bottle, now lying peacefully in the heather.

They went through all the gardens, and everywhere the mess was the same. The only new thing they found was a gob of purple chewing gum in the raspberries behind "Vale End"—and that didn't cheer them much.

At lunchtime each went his own way to think things over in the shade of a convenient tree. And if snoring and thinking are at all the same thing—which perhaps they are—they thought very carefully and conscientiously all afternoon.

Later that day, they had a town meeting, at a long table under the mulberry tree in Cricket's garden. The meeting was to decide: What ought to be done. Who ought to do it. And how.

First they agreed to put all the rubbish together in one big pile outside town. Spider suggested that they burn the lot. But how do you burn a tin can and a pie pan and a clear glass bottle?

Moth suggested that they dig a hole big enough for everything and bury it.

"That would mean a *lot* of digging. And I mean a LOT!" said Cricket. "Besides, it's such a waste— if only we could think of a way."

Then the brown beetle got up, tapped politely on his teacup with his spoon, and said that he had a plan.

This is his plan (known later as The Hon. Wm. Beetle's Garbage Emergency Plan): (1) Most of the stuff dumped on us is reusable. (2) Some is perishable and should be handled first. (3) Cut perishables into suitable pieces. (4) Wrap in tinfoil, or candy wrapper, and store. (5) Sort out remaining stuff, plastic tubes, etc., and stack for later use. (6) Repair damaged mushrooms. (7) Clean up!

"While doing this," said Beetle, "we'll have plenty of time to decide what to do with the tubes, the tin can, and the rest."

When Beetle sat down, there was a burst of applause, and Snail—having nothing to applaud with —said, "Bravo!" in his deep bass voice.

Then the meeting broke up, and they all went to work.

News of the disaster at Mushroom Center had spread throughout the woods, and friends and relatives began pouring in to ask for news and offer their help, if help should be needed.

Long trestle tables had been set up on the Common, and at the tables stood the townspeople and their friends and second cousins, cutting, wrapping and talking.

Moth's nieces were there, and Cricket's nephews,

Ladybug's four ladylike sisters, and Spider's two spidery brothers.

Beetle had been joined by acquaintances from the woods and the river. Caterpillar's cousins had rallied to her in great numbers.

Snail's relatives, as might be expected, turned up later.

There had never been so many people in Mushroom Center, and they all worked hard. Even the ladylike sisters rolled up their sleeves and pitched in.

By the end of the day, all that was perishable had been cut and sliced and scooped up and divided and pickled and cooked and potted and wrapped and labeled and stored, till there wasn't a cupboard or closet or box or drawer in all of Mushroom Center that wasn't bursting with provisions.

The dill pickle had been cut into two thousand seven hundred and forty-nine pieces and put up in two hundred and thirty-two jars, fourteen bowls, and a jug. It had taken a gang of eleven tumblebugs (friends of Beetle) three hours and thirteen minutes to get the pickle out of Moth's chimney, using absolutely no end of ropes and pulleys. So much for statistics.

At the end of the second day, most of the friends

and acquaintances and nearly all the relatives returned home, each carrying provisions for a month.

A few stayed on, helping wherever they could and sleeping in odd nooks and corners when the day's work was done.

One by one the mushrooms were righted and the fences mended.

One by one the gardens were cleared, the lawns cut and raked, the lanes swept, and the hedges trimmed.

New glass was put in the windows, new wax was put on the floors, and everything in need of a brush or sponge or rag was rubbed and scrubbed and polished, till the whole village sparkled like a soap bubble and smelled deliciously of beeswax and ammonia water.

Everyday at lunch (and again after supper), they had a meeting, and at every meeting they made plans and discussed them and argued about them and

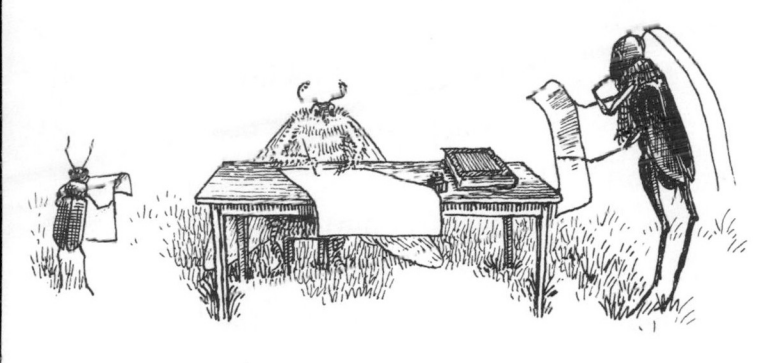

turned them upside down and inside out—which, of course, is what meetings are for.

And while they talked, Moth wrote everything down in her shadowy little hand. This is what she wrote:

How to use cigarette butts: Cut cork on filter into pieces suitable for doormats or floor tiles. Cut spongy part of filter into thick slices, cover with fabric and use as pillows. Cut paper into squares, fold, and use for napkins or letter paper. Dry tobacco and use as fuel in stoves and fireplaces. Use ashes as fertilizer (if suitable).

Pie Pan: Paint blue inside, fill with water, and use as pool. Or, paint white inside, put upside down on pieces of drinking straws, and use as band shell.

Ice-cream sticks: Cut into pieces—for tabletops, boxes, chests, cupboards, floors and doors.

Bottle: Use, lying on its side, dug halfway into ground, and half filled with dirt, as greenhouse. Use fireflies for illumination.

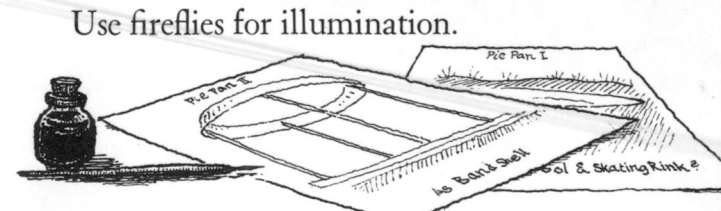

36

Then: Make greenhouse and pool part of small park.

Perhaps: Pool could be used as skating rink in the winter.

They had many other ideas, some of which Moth wrote down, and some of which she left out because —believe me—they were quite silly.

Spider suggested that the straws could be cut into sections for use as barber shop poles. No one thought much of that.

Someone thought they could fill the can with dirt and use it as a giant roller. To roll what? Or they could dig it into the ground and dump their garbage

into it through the triangular hole in the top.

As for the purple gum! No one even wanted to think of it.

"It's strange," said Beetle, one evening when he and Cricket were sitting by the fire in Parson's Cottage, "but that tin can, all those straws, and that mess of purple gum—somehow it suggests something quite simple—if only I could think of it. You do know what I mean, don't you, Cricket?"

"Oh, I do indeed!" said Cricket, but he didn't, so they talked about other things, till the fire died down in the grate and Beetle went home.

Cricket went to bed and fell asleep almost immediately, but Beetle sat down in his easy chair with a bit of paper and a pencil. And part of the night he did calculations in his head, and part of the night he wrote them down on his paper to see why they didn't come out right. Then he said: "Yes, of course—" and "How silly of me to forget—" until his paper was full of figures, and his head was empty, and the sun came up, and he went to bed.

Beetle arrived a little late for their next town meeting, carrying a small bunch of papers. He put the papers on the table in front of him and, when he had sorted them out, got up to introduce his Plan for the Use of THE TIN CAN, THE DRINKING STRAWS, and THE PURPLE CHEWING GUM. They all listened with the gravest attention.

"Place TIN CAN on low circular stone wall, cover with pine needle shingles and use as WATER TOWER. Use ice-cream sticks to construct windmill for pumping water from spring into tower. Use DRINKING STRAWS for pipes, to pipe water into every single mushroom in Mushroom Center! Use PURPLE CHEWING GUM to glue pipes together and keep them tight. P.S. If there is enough water, we might even have a fountain in the middle of the pool."

The plan was accompanied by some very wonderful little drawings of waterworks, windmills, pipes and fountains, and the most astonishing calculations concerning watersheds and watertables and how to construct a pump.

They elected Beetle Waterworks Commissioner on the spot. And he accepted.

When work began the following day, some enterprising earthworms offered to do the plumbing. A firm of carpenter ants undertook construction and shingling. Caterpillars, fitted with little scoops, did earth removal. Spider spun ropes for hoisting. Snail

—slow but dependable—did the hoisting. Moth carried shingles to the ants. Firefly and her two younger brothers worked in the greenhouse. Ladybug produced tea, toast, and strawberry jam for everybody. And while they all worked, Cricket played encouraging music for them.

When the tower was on its foundation, and the pipes were in the ground, when the pool was full of water, and the greenhouse full of flowers, they put a stairway on the tower and a railing around the edge at the top. From there, a splendid view could be had of the town, the Fern Woods, the Mole Hills and —on clear days—even Robin's Rock and Turnpike's End.

But by then, they were all too exhausted to climb stairs and celebrated the day by not having a single town meeting either before lunch or after supper. Instead, they stayed home, turning their water taps on and off all afternoon.

But Beetle went down to the river to a friend he had who was a water bug, and they spent the day together fishing the pools below the rapids.

Later in the week, when they were all rested, they had an evening party in the park, with speeches and balloons and colored lights in the trees. And at exactly midnight, a display of fireworks from the top of the tower.

After that things returned to normal. They all had their own things to look after. Some puttered about in their gardens in the low autumn sunshine. Some stacked their firewood. Some brought in their apples.

In the garden of cabbages and roses, only a single bloom was left and when that died, it was summer's end. The days grew darker, the nights grew colder. The leaves came off the trees and at last the ground froze.

But in the greenhouse, summer lingered on, and the fireflies kept busy, watering and pruning and making displays of late-blooming asters.

If you should ever come to that part of the woods on a snowy afternoon, look out for the Turnpike and the Common. Where they meet is the entrance to the park.

The greenhouse is lit by fireflies casting a warm glow over the rink, where the friends skate together. The snail has four skates tied on him and glides over the ice with much grace.

When they tire of skating, they all gather in the greenhouse around a teapot that never gets cold.

And there we will leave them now, under their green ferns, in the heart of winter.